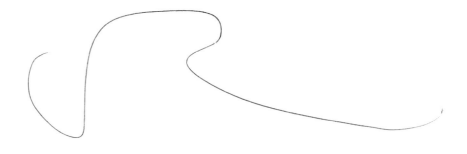

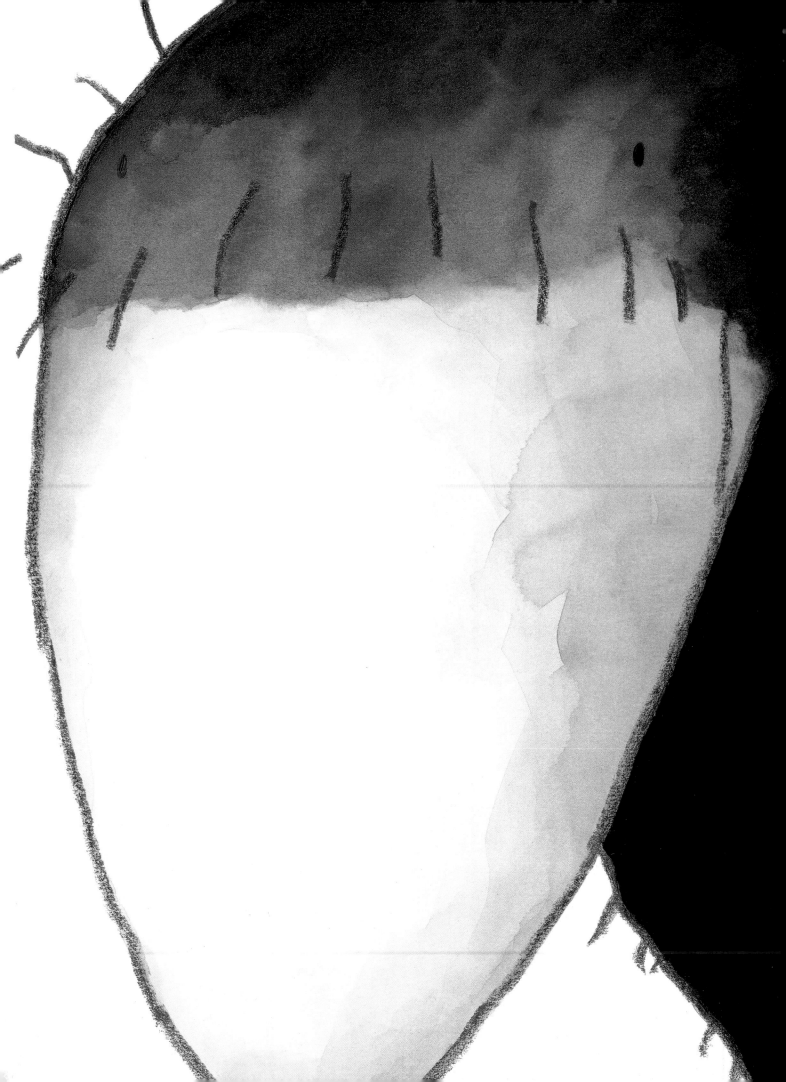

Rafik Schami

# The Crow Who
# Stood on His Beak

Illustrated by Els Cools
and Oliver Streich

Translated by Anthea Bell

North-South Books
New York / London

ONCE UPON A TIME a great many crows lived in an old walnut tree. The tree used to have plenty of room for them all, but as the years went by branches and twigs became brittle and dropped off. However, none of the crows thought that was any reason to move away into the forest. It was dark in the forest, and they wouldn't have such a good view from the trees there as they had from the big walnut tree, which stood by itself in a field.

In one of the nests in the walnut tree a little crow lived alone with his mother. Soon after he had hatched from his egg, his father had been killed by a mighty eagle.

The little crow's mother had to find food for him by herself, so he was often left all alone in his nest. When he was bored he would climb out, hop through the branches, and visit the other crow children. Their parents angrily shooed him away.

"That lad's mother has nothing to crow about, letting him stray like that!" they cawed. They were upset, because their own children wanted to leave the nest and hop from branch to branch, just like the little crow.

Whatever the weather, rain or shine, the little crow played all day long. He ventured a little farther every day.

Sometimes he hopped too far, and tumbled to the ground. He called for help, but the other crows cawed scornfully, "Your legs carried you down, your wings can carry you up again!" So then the little crow had to wait for his mother to come home and help him into the nest.

"Don't worry, your wings will soon be strong enough for you to help yourself," his mother comforted her son, stroking his head.

The little crow kept thinking up new games. One day he turned upside down and stood on his beak. If he spread his wings he could balance on his beak for quite a while.

"Hooray!" cawed all the crow children.

And soon the walnut tree was filled with the excited, happy shouting of the children and the horrified screeches of their parents as all the young crows tried standing on their beaks, churning up the nests badly.

"The boy's crazy!" said a powerful father crow. "Standing on his beak like that, setting our children a bad example! I ask you! His head is full of nonsense!"

"Children need to play," the little crow's mother defended her son.

One day the little crow heard a grandmother crow telling her grandchildren, "Be good and stop trying to stand on your beaks, and I'll tell you a story."

Since children love stories, and they know grannies have good hearts but bad memories, the young crows promised never to stand on their beaks again. Granny Crow cleared her throat, and the little crow settled down to listen, like her own three grandchildren.

*"Once upon a time there was a crow who lived happily with the other crows. One day he heard of the peacock, the king of the birds. The peacock is the loveliest bird on earth. He can spread his magnificent feathers into a fan more beautiful than the sun or the moon. His tail captivates the world. Well, this crow wanted to captivate his own friends, so he went to see the peacock, who lived in his royal meadow beyond the dark forest. After a long, hard journey the crow arrived and admired the peacock. He took a deep breath, puffed out his chest, craned his neck, and tried to walk proudly, following the peacock step by step.*

*"'You silly bird!' said the peacock to his follower. 'A crow is still a crow even if he puffs himself out!'*

*"But the crow kept trying. He felt dreadfully stiff because it isn't easy for crows to walk like peacocks. However, after many days he could strut about like the king of birds.*

"'Well,' he said to himself, 'maybe I can't spread my short tail into a fan, but I can strut about with my head held high just like a peacock.' He went back to the crows and marched up and down in front of them. But they just laughed at the crow when he kept cawing, 'Look, look! See how proudly I can walk?'

"'Careful you don't burst!' some of the birds jeered, and others asked him spitefully, 'Did you swallow a melon?'

"The crow's back and chest hurt, but his friends' mockery hurt most of all. After a few days he gave up imitating the peacock and tried to walk like a crow again. But he had forgotten how. So he took one step like a crow and the next like a peacock, and the other crows laughed at him more than ever. And the crow lived unhappily ever after," Granny Crow finished her story.

"Does the peacock keep his tail spread all day long?" asked the little crow, thinking about it.

"Yes, all day long," said Granny Crow.

"That's boring! What else does he do?"

Granny Crow looked at the little crow quite crossly. "He is the king of the birds and only he can fan out his tail, and that's enough. Go away now, do!"

The little crow left Granny Crow's nest. He spent all day think-ing. When his mother came home that evening, she found, to her surprise, that her son didn't even want any supper.

 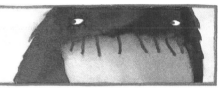

"Mother, why does the peacock spread his tail?" he asked.

"He just does, son. He was born a king!"

"I want to visit the peacock and ask him why he does it."

His mother saw her son's shining eyes and began to shed tears.

"But you can't fly. Wild animals will eat you. Think of what hap-pened to your poor father! Stay here and don't make me unhappy," she begged sadly.

Day after day went by, and the little crow felt more and more restless.

By night he dreamed of growing strong wings and flying over the forest and the high mountains.

But by day he just flapped his wings helplessly a couple of times and kept falling to the ground.

One morning, however, the little crow decided he simply had to visit the peacock. He didn't wait for his mother to come home, because he felt helpless when she cried. So he just said good-bye to the other crows and set out.

"Poor fool. It serves his silly mother right," he heard the other crows say.

He still couldn't fly properly, so he hopped a few steps, fluttered a little way, hopped again, and then had a rest so that he could fly a little way once more. About midday he came to the dark forest.

"If only I had strong wings, I could fly over the forest," he sighed, quivering with fright. "Well, I'll have to go through it." Plucking up all his courage, he hopped in among the trees.

"What do I sssee here?" hissed a snake suddenly. It was lying in a little clearing, basking in the sun.

"Who are you?" asked the little crow in surprise. He had never seen a snake before.

"I am every crow'sss friend. Come here and let me kisss you!" whispered the snake, gulping greedily, because its mouth was watering. The little crow jumped in alarm.

"But you don't have any wings. What are those sharp, pointy things in your beak?" he asked suspiciously, looking at the snake's fangs.

"Oh, those are my jewelsss," the snake told the little crow, slowly slithering in his direction.

"Stop!" said the crow, taking a couple of steps back. "Don't come any closer. Your jewels frighten me. Take them off before you kiss me."

"I was going to give them to you. Wear them on your neck and you'll be the finest crow for miles around," whispered the snake enticingly.

"But I don't want to wear any jewels on my neck!" insisted the little crow, and he hurried on again, leaving the snake behind him, cursing.

The forest floor was covered with branches and dead tree trunks, and the crow had difficulty getting over them all. He stumbled, got up again, said some rude words, and went on once more. After hours of toil and trouble, he came to the meadows beyond the dark forest.

He flew up to the top of a fir tree for a better view, and was surprised to find he could easily reach the highest branch of the mighty tree. His wings had grown stronger from all his efforts in the forest. The green meadows below went on and on and on.

In the distance, he saw a flock of white doves arguing. When the crow asked them the way, they stopped arguing and began to laugh. "Another crow wanting to see the peacock!" Then they continued their bickering.

"I'm the prettiest white dove of all!" cooed one of them.

"You think you're the prettiest?" said another dove, interrupting. "Why, you have two feathers missing from your right wing and one from your left wing. Now just look at my wings! Aren't they magnificent?" And the dove flapped its wings proudly. Not a feather was missing.

"You, the prettiest? Don't make me laugh!" cried a third. It had a ragged tail. "You have a bald patch!" it chuckled nastily, pointing scornfully at the second dove's head, which was covered with scars.

"You just hold your beak! Look at your raggletaggle tail!"

And squabbling again, the doves began pecking at each other.

The crow flew on, shaking his head in surprise.

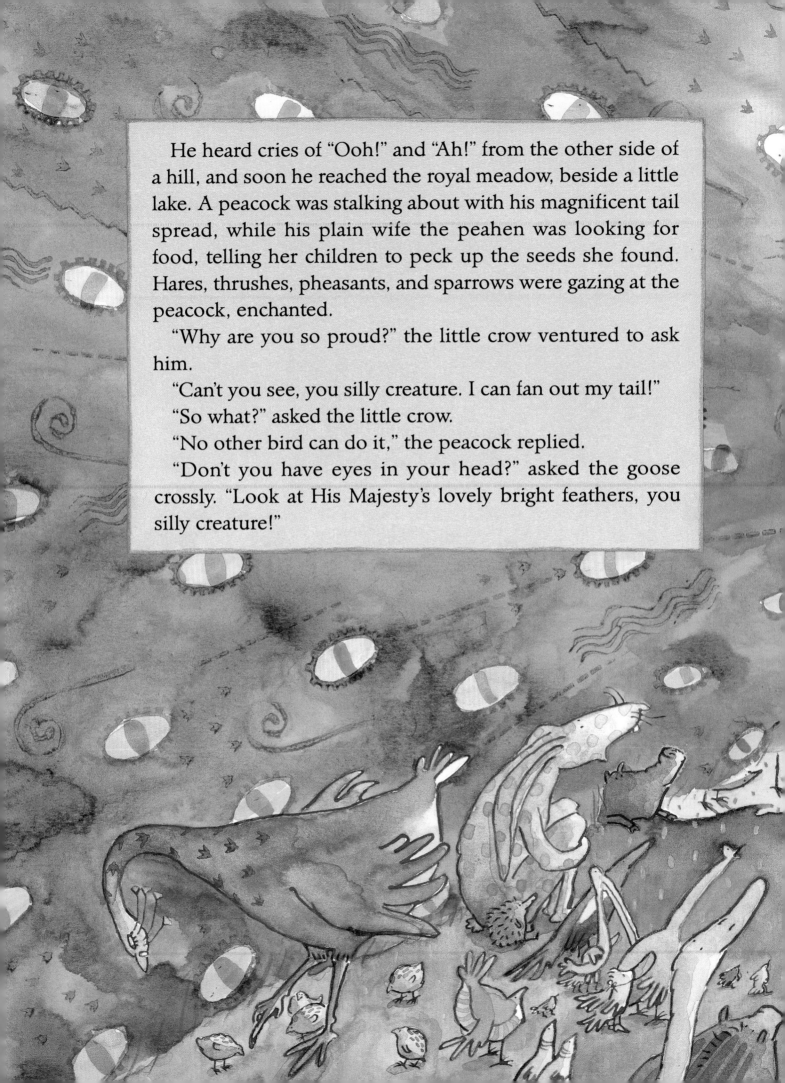

He heard cries of "Ooh!" and "Ah!" from the other side of a hill, and soon he reached the royal meadow, beside a little lake. A peacock was stalking about with his magnificent tail spread, while his plain wife the peahen was looking for food, telling her children to peck up the seeds she found. Hares, thrushes, pheasants, and sparrows were gazing at the peacock, enchanted.

"Why are you so proud?" the little crow ventured to ask him.

"Can't you see, you silly creature. I can fan out my tail!"

"So what?" asked the little crow.

"No other bird can do it," the peacock replied.

"Don't you have eyes in your head?" asked the goose crossly. "Look at His Majesty's lovely bright feathers, you silly creature!"

"But every bird is beautiful in its own way!" said the crow.

"Well, you're the same dull black all over!" laughed the peacock.

"So? Can you do anything but fan out your tail? Do you know any games the others could play too?" asked the crow.

"I can do anything!" boasted the peacock.

"Can you stand on your beak?"

"Stand on my beak?" repeated the peacock in surprise.

"That's right, your beak," said the little crow, nodding.

He stuck his beak in the sand and kicked his thin legs up in the air. Then he flapped his wings to help him keep his balance.

"Amazing!" cried the magpies.

"Terrific!" the sparrows applauded.

"Fabulous!" grunted a young wild boar.

"Nothing easier!" said the peacock jealously, and tried. With a squawk, he fell on his back, bending three of his long tail feathers. "The wind blew me over!" he cried furiously, spreading his tail.

But next time he tried he fell over again, bending two more of his lovely long feathers, and his crown was all untidy. The little crow cawed with amusement when the peacock fanned his tail once more. It looked terrible with those bent feathers.

Now a number of birds turned upside down on the grass and tried to stand on their beaks. The sparrows could do it easily, the goose fell flat on her face, and the magpies chattered crossly because the pheasant had stumbled over them just as they almost had the trick of it.

"This is all nonsense. Why don't you admire my tail instead?" cried the angry peacock, stalking up and down in front of them in a flustered way.

But none of the birds were interested in him anymore, not even the peahen. She thought the game was great fun, and laughed when she kept falling over. She was delighted when her youngest chick managed to stand on its beak.

"It may be nonsense, but it's more fun that just admiring you the whole time," said the little crow, laughing when he too fell flat on the ground. He'd forgotten not to open his beak while he was standing on it.

"Such impertinence! I'll teach you a lesson!" cried the peacock, running after the little crow, who hastily disappeared into a bramble bush. In his fury the peacock was caught up in the thorny shoots, so that he could go neither backward nor forward.

However, the little crow came out on the other side.

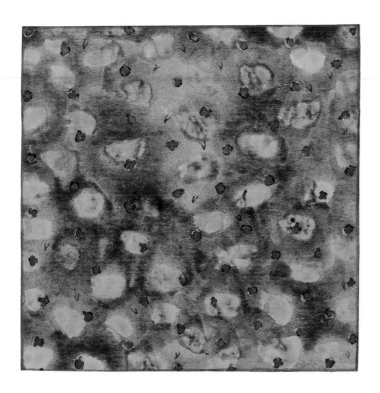

"We must help him!" he cried, plucking a long feather from the peacock's tail. The other birds joined in, plucking feathers from the peacock too. They helped him get out of the bramble bush backward. Furiously, the peacock screamed and tried to spread his tail.

The birds laughed at the sight of his plucked behind.

"You look like a roast chicken!" cried the peahen and she joined in the laughter too.

The birds thought up lots of amusing games to play with his feathers.

They used the feathers . . .

to tickle each other,

fan each other,

and decorate     each other.

But the little crow chose one of the
beautiful feathers and took it home as
fast as he could go.

His mother was delighted to see him home again safe and sound, and she loved his beautiful present. Proudly she decorated her nest with it. She kissed her son, stroked his head for a long time, and listened to his story.

Many of the crow children hopped out of their nests and came to hear the brave little crow tell his tale too.

Since then, the peacock has never kept his tail spread all day long. He only fans out his feathers for a very short time, screaming aloud as he does so because he remembers that dreadful day.

And he takes very good care that there isn't a crow anywhere near.

Copyright © 1996 by Nord-Süd Verlag AG, Gossau Zürich, Switzerland.
First published in Switzerland under the title *Der Schnabelsteher*.
English translation copyright © 1996 by North-South Books Inc.
All rights reserved. First published in the United States, Great Britain, Canada,
Australia, and New Zealand in 1996 by North-South Books, an imprint of
Nord-Süd Verlag AG, Gossau Zürich, Switzerland.
Distributed in the United States by North-South Books Inc., New York.

ISBN 1-55858-527-3 (trade binding)
1 3 5 7 9 TB 10 8 6 4 2
ISBN 1-55858-528-1 (library binding)
1 3 5 7 9 LB 10 8 6 4 2
Printed in Germany

LIBRARY OF CONGRESS CATALOGING-IN-PUBLICATION DATA.
Schami, Rafik. 1946-
[Schnabelsteher. English]
The crow who stood on his beak/ Rafki Schami;
illustrated by Els Cools and Oliver Streich; translated by Anthea Bell.
Summary: An adventurous little crow goes in search of the magnificent peacock,
and, upon meting him, manages to humble the peacock
and endear himself to the other birds.
[1. Crows—Fiction. 2. Peacocks—Fiction. 3. Birds—Fiction.]
I. Cools, Els, ill.  II. Streich, Oliver, ill.  III. Bell, Anthea.  IV. Title.
PZ7.S3337Cr  1996
[Fic]—dc20    95-36756

A CIP catalogue record for this book is available
from The British Library.